For Amy, the light of my day x – J.B.

For Mum and Dad W, with love xx And for Christian, always – C.J-I.

First published 2017 by Macmillan Children's Books
an imprint of Pan Macmillan,
20 New Wharf Road, London N1 9RR
Associated companies throughout the world

www.panmacmillan.com

ISBN: 978-1-5098-3439-6 (HB)
ISBN: 978-1-5098-3440-2 (PB)

1 3 5 7 9 8 6 4 2

A CIP catalogue record for this book is available from the British Library.

Printed in China

Written by
James Brown

Illustrated by
Cally Johnson-Isaacs

MACMILLAN CHILDREN'S BOOKS

Days with my mummy are always such fun,
the sun's woken up, there's so much to get done!
Together it's special, all laughter and play,
because Mummy is always the light of my day.

In the morning we're speedy at getting up quickly,
I have to watch out, Mummy knows that I'm tickly!

"Let's count down from ten!" she shouts, racing so fast –

but where is my teddy? Who saw him last?

Mummy's so super at doing the shopping,

we zoom round the shops without even stopping!

Lifting bag after bag, Mummy's ever so strong,

she lifts me up too when the walk home's too long.

My mummy is gentle, so caring and kind.
We walk through the park and look down to find . . .

A poor little ladybird's stuck on its back,
but Mummy soon helps it turn right back on track.

With Mummy the roundabout whirls around faster,

until I fall off and cry, “I need a plaster!”

Mummy kisses and rubs and the hurt goes away,
then she gives me a hug and we run off to play.

My favourite things are baking and cooking –
and licking the spoon when Mummy's not looking!
I sprinkle the sprinkles and make a big mess,
then Mummy joins in and makes *her* cake the best.

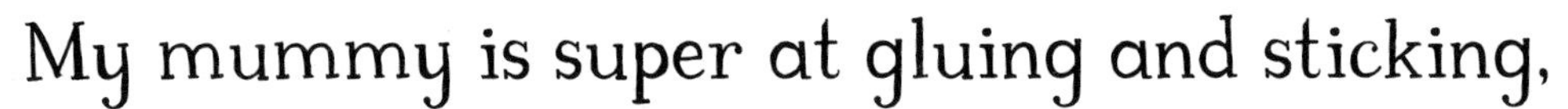

My mummy is super at gluing and sticking,

at mending and bending

and sorting and picking.

She can save any toy from certain disaster,
there's no one on earth who can fix my things faster.

The washing's a rainbow we love to hang out,
it's really good fun for a quick kick-about.

In no time at all, everything's dry
and the bed sheets are capes so we take off and fly!

Mummy knows when it's time to make me some food,
my tummy is rumbly, I'm in a bad mood.
"Don't grumble," she smiles, "your dinner is ready.
You'll soon have your favourite . . .

and so will your teddy!"

We have so much fun playing splash in the bath,
Mummy tickles my tummy and makes us both laugh.

She holds out the towel with her arms open wide

and wraps me up safe, feeling snuggly inside.

With Mummy I cuddle up closely in bed,
she makes sure I'm comfy and kisses my head.

She reads me adventures, we wave to the moon,
then I drift off to sleep as she sings me a tune.

Days with my mummy are always such fun,
and ever so special together, as one.
I can't wait for tomorrow, more laughter and play,
because Mummy is always the light of my day.